Anyone who argues by referring to authority is not using his mind but rather his memory.

Science is the captain, and practice the soldiers. Those who fall in love with practice without science
are like a sailor who enters a ship without a helm or compass, and who never can be certain whither he is going.

Instrumental or mechanical science is of all the noblest and the most useful,
seeing that by means of this all animated bodies that have movement perform all their actions.

St. Andrew's night, I am through with squaring the circle; and this was the end of the light,
and of the night, and of the paper I was writing on; this conclusion has come to me at the end of the last hour.

Let no one read me who is not a mathematician.

You will take the measure of all the muscles and learn their functions, who moves them, and how they are implemented.

While man has within himself bones as a stay and framework for the flesh,
the world has stones which are the supports of earth.
While man has within him a pool of blood wherein the lungs as he breathes expand and contract,
so the body of the earth has its ocean, which also rises and falls every six hours with the breathing of the world.

Study the science of art and the art of science.

Which is better—to draw from nature or from the antique?

The mind of the painter should be like a mirror which always takes the color of the thing that it reflects,
and which is filled by as many images as there are things placed before it.

Go every Saturday to the public bathhouse. You will see nudes there....
Cristofano da Casti, who is at the Pietà, has a fine head...Giovanna has a fantastic face.

The most important consideration in painting is that the movements
of each figure express its mental state, such as desire, scorn, anger, pity, and the like.

A good painter has two chief objects to paint, man and the intention of the soul; the former is easy, the latter hard.

If you do not rest upon the good foundation of nature, you will labor with little honor and less profit. Those who take for their standards anyone but nature—the mistress of all masters - weary themselves in vain.

ROBERT BYRD

Leonardo

BEAUTIFUL DREAMER

Dutton Children's Books
NEW YORK

LEONARDO

Think back to the last time you were trying to follow an explanation of how something complicated, like a bird's wing or a poem or the human eye, actually worked. Or perhaps you once tried to draw a leaf or a horse's head or a hand, making every detail exact. Many people—perhaps most—are more than willing to skip the hard parts and rely on someone else's understanding. After all, solving an intricate puzzle or problem can be tough going. And yet, it can also be exhilarating.

Five hundred years ago, a man lived and worked who thrived on the "hard parts." A painter and engineer, he wasn't content simply to accept other people's explanations. He wanted to figure things out for himself—everything! How birds fly. How we see. What makes the blood move in the body. What gives an arch its strength or the sky its depth. How to make a painting alive with emotion, reality, mystery. He did not ignore what others had learned. Though largely self-taught, he was a voracious reader and conversed with mathematicians, architects, artists, monks, scholars, and kings. But he explored whether their knowledge would help him answer *his* questions, whether it agreed with *his* understanding. For him, studying nature directly held the key. With his patient, deep powers of observation, he divined nature's laws and used them to design unimagined marvels. He was so curious and so intense about his investigations—and so ambitious in his undertakings—that he often left a project unfinished to take up a new one.

This man was Leonardo da Vinci, and he was born in a remarkable period of European culture known as the Renaissance, or "rebirth." Artists and scholars, merchants and politicians were bursting with the desire to glorify human achievement in the spirit of the ancient Greeks and Romans. But it was also a dangerous period. People lived at the mercy of plagues, harsh weather, brutal rulers. War was constant. Few could read or write, and most were suspicious of what they did not understand. Though sought-after as a brilliant painter, in his scientific investigations Leonardo often felt it necessary to work in secret and alone. Who would believe all that he could fathom? Although not all his theories were correct, many of his studies anticipated science and technology that today we take for granted.

To his students, Leonardo counseled respect for beauty, goodness, and truth. All life was interconnected, he felt. He championed the potential of even the humblest among us to question and create, and so to achieve the most beautiful of our dreams.

The earth is moved from its position by the weight of a tiny bird alighting upon it.

The surface of the sea is moved by a small drop of water falling upon it.

"*This writing in detail about the kites seems to be my destiny, for among my earliest childhood memories, it seemed to me that, as I lay in my cradle, a kite flew down and opened my mouth with its tail, and struck me several times with its tail inside my lips.*" These few lines describing a childhood memory of Leonardo's are rare. Although thousands of pages of Leonardo's notes survive to the present day, most involve his artistic development or scientific investigations—he was seldom personal in his writings. His interest in kites comes up in regard to his later obsession with flight.

·Vinci·

·Florence·

More than five hundred years ago, a remarkable child was born near the town of Vinci in the sun-drenched Italian countryside. One morning as he lay in his cradle, a silver bird of prey swooped down very close to the baby boy. The fierce bird circled around the crib, causing great alarm. His mother and the villagers came running to protect the baby. But Leonardo, as the boy came to be called, was not afraid. Even as a child, he seemed to possess unusual powers of awareness and intelligence. He reached out as if to touch the bird's great wings, and he smiled as he watched the beautifully feathered creature fly up, up, and out of sight.

The bird Leonardo saw as a young child is called a kite. Graceful, hawklike kites can still be spotted in the mountains of Italy. They are known for their ability to glide effortlessly on the wind for long periods of time. Man-made kites are named for them.

Milan

Genoa

Milan

Venice

Vinci

Florence

Corsica

Rome

Sardinia

Naples

ITALY

Sicily

Leonardo collected specimens of all kinds—rocks, plants, insects, and small animals—and he began to draw them. He felt he might better understand how things were formed and how they really worked by carefully recording their images. He made drawings that astonished everyone with their beauty and detail.

Even as a child, he marveled at the movement of animals and clouds, the patterns of light and shade on objects, and the motion of water.

When he was very young, Leonardo probably lived with his mother, Caterina, a simple peasant. His father, Ser Piero, came from a long line of important landowners and public officials. Ser Piero did not remain in the town of Vinci or marry Caterina. Educated and ambitious, he set out to make his fortune in the city of Florence.

After a few years, Leonardo's mother married another man and had children with him. Leonardo was taken into the comfortable farmhouse where his father had grown up, to be raised by his grandfather and his uncle Francesco. Because his parents had never married, Leonardo was not allowed to receive a formal education. He could not look forward to becoming a notary, like his father, or to holding any high office. Nor could he inherit the family land. Instead, he

would have to find another path for himself in the world.

Leonardo learned to read and write, but his true interest lay in observing the world around him. A solitary boy, he spent countless days roaming the hilly countryside near his home. He would follow a turtle and wonder how it crawled along so slowly in its shell. Why were the rabbit's ears so long? He reached to touch a frog, and it leaped away. How did it move so quickly? He drifted in the pools and streams around Vinci and learned to swim by moving his arms and legs like the frogs. He watched the birds flying overhead and studied the fish swimming below. How their fins were like little wings! How effortlessly the bats darted off at dusk, beating their wings against the summer sky. If he could learn to swim by copying a frog, could humans learn to fly by studying birds?

Leonardo's young uncle Francesco greatly admired nature's beauty and taught Leonardo what he could about plants and animals, about how the sun and moon rise and set, and about changes in the seasons and weather. But Leonardo's desire to understand the world around him was never satisfied. Soon he was asking questions that no one could answer.

He saw storm clouds in the distance and wondered why lightning would flash before thunder sounded. He dropped a stone into a pool and wondered what made circles move outward from the splash. Ducks floating on the water swam away as he approached. How did they skim so smoothly over the surface while his stone always sank straight to the bottom? Once Leonardo watched as a storm flooded his valley, destroying farms and homes. The sight left him with a lifelong awe and respect for the power of water.

The hills around Vinci were studded with craggy rocks and shadowy caves. One afternoon Leonardo came upon the entrance to a cave and ventured inside. A still, eerie darkness surprised and frightened him. But his curiosity drove him forward, deeper into the cave, where he found a great pile of bleached bones and shells.

Were the bones from an ancient monster? Or from some colossal fish? But how could seashells be found high in the hills, so far from the sea? Had the ocean risen there long ago, when the pile of bones was still a living creature?

Leonardo would travel far from Vinci and his uncle Francesco, but for the rest of his life he observed the world around him with the same awe and delight that he felt as a boy. Nature inspired his curiosity, and the answers he found there would inspire his genius.

"If you throw a stone into a pond…all the waves which strike against these shores are thrown back to where the stone struck."

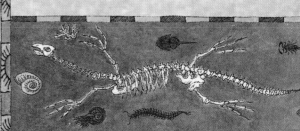

"How can it carry the shells, mollusks, snails, and similar things from the bottom of the sea and leave them upon the shore?"

"I ventured among the gloomy rocks. And after I had remained there awhile, suddenly two emotions arose in me, fear and desire; fear of the threatening and dark cavern, desire to see whether there were any marvelous things within."

When he died, the childless Francesco left his estate to Leonardo, as he would have to a son.

When Leonardo was in his teens, he left the sleepy village of Vinci to join his father in Florence.

Less than a day's journey from the village, life in this magnificent, prosperous city must have seemed a whole universe away to Leonardo. Florence teemed with merchants selling goods from all over the known world. Jugglers, musicians, and peasants with donkey carts jammed the crowded alleyways, while throngs of elegantly dressed nobles and their ladies paraded through the streets.

Renaissance Florence was an independent state, with its own government, culture, army, and even its own money. The wealthy Medicis, the most powerful family in the city, were renowned as lovers of art. Sculptors, philosophers, painters, scientists, poets, and architects—with the support of the Medicis, all were encouraged to live in Florence and through their work to make the city exciting and beautiful.

Leonardo was said to be tall and handsome, charming and

In the center of the city, the construction of a magnificent cathedral called the duomo had been under way for centuries. Machines designed by a brilliant architect named Brunelleschi made it possible to lift the heavy materials that would be used to construct the towering structure's

Leonardo bought birds in cages in the marketplace and released them in a room so that he could study their movement. When he had studied and sketched long enough, crowds would gather and watch in amazement as Leonardo set the birds free.

massive red dome. Young Leonardo was intrigued and inspired by these devices. It was the beginning of a lifelong interest in mechanics and technology. Brunelleschi's great dome, a wonderful accomplishment of Renaissance architecture, still dominates the skyline of Florence.

Over the centuries Florence was home to remarkable artists. Some of the best-known were: Dante the poet, Giotto the painter, and Leonardo's rival, Michelangelo. Within a short distance, Leonardo could see the works of the architect Alberti and the sculptor Donatello.

fashionably dressed, and so strong he could impress people with seemingly superhuman feats, like bending iron horseshoes with his bare hands. He soon became a familiar figure in the city, sketching objects that interested him and studying the paintings and architecture of Florence's elegant churches and public squares.

Ser Piero decided to show his son's sketches to Andrea del Verrocchio, a famed sculptor and master craftsman whose prestigious workshop produced much of the fine arts of wealthy Florentine society. Verrocchio must have seen talent in the drawings. When Leonardo was about 14, he moved into the master artisan's studio to begin his training as an apprentice.

Here in this bustling city of culture and art, Leonardo would spend the next 12 years of his life in the workshop of Verrocchio. The boy from Vinci could not have found a better place in all the world to investigate and explore, to ask questions and to learn.

Andrea del Verrocchio

Andrea del Verrocchio is probably best known for his statue of *David*, from the biblical story of David and Goliath. The slender sculpture was made while Leonardo worked with Verrocchio, and an old rumor exists that the peaceful face of the youthful David is modeled on Leonardo. Verrocchio and his apprentice collaborated on a painting called *Baptism of Christ*. A biblical scene, it shows two angels kneeling at the feet of Christ and John the Baptist. Master artists of the Renaissance often completed only part of a work, allowing students to fill in the details. Verrocchio left the final angel in *Baptism of Christ* to his apprentice. Leonardo's angel, gazing in adoration at Christ, is remarkable for its soft, expressive beauty. The 16th-century biographer Vasari wrote that Verrocchio gave up painting when he saw it, for the teacher knew his pupil had outdone him. *"Poor is the pupil who does not surpass his master,"* wrote Leonardo.

Florence had more respect for artists than other Italian cities, but fine arts such as painting were still considered less important than liberal arts, such as mathematics or philosophy. As a result, some artists never bothered to sign their work, and many of the talented craftsmen who made Florence beautiful are unknown to us.

Leonardo was one of many apprentices who lived and studied in Verrocchio's workshop. Maestro Verrocchio taught Leonardo every aspect of his craft. At first the young man swept floors, ran errands, and practiced drawing. Soon he learned to prepare canvases, make brushes, grind paints, and mix colors. Leonardo also sculpted in wood and clay, and studied metalwork in gold, silver, and bronze.

At that time, an artist acquired many skills in order to satisfy the fanciful orders of patrons, or customers. In Verrocchio's workshop, Leonardo began to fashion furniture for wealthy homes, costumes for carnivals, and to make musical instruments and even surgical tools. He studied mathematics so that he could understand perspective, a technique used to create an illusion of space and depth in paintings, whereby scenes drawn on flat canvases appear three-dimensional. He studied the anatomy of people and animals in order to make his figures look lively and real.

In the busy workshop, teams of artists worked on long and complicated projects. An altarpiece, marble statues, jewelry, architectural plans for a palace, or lovely floats for the celebration of a marriage might all be under way at the same time. Immersed in the creative energy of the Renaissance, Leonardo soon excelled in all of the arts, especially painting, and found Verrocchio trusting him with more and more challenging tasks.

In 1472, when he was about 20, Leonardo officially graduated from apprentice to master artist. However, the new "maestro" remained in the friendly workshop of Verrocchio for several more years, helping younger artists and working with Verrocchio on many important pieces of art.

Although he was a prodigy in the studio, outshining his fellow students in both skill and imagination, Leonardo's early career as a painter did not go particularly well. Throughout his life, Leonardo would become so absorbed in new ideas that he would have trouble finishing many projects, including his first commissions for paintings and sculptures in Florence. Perhaps this is one reason why, when he was about 30 years old, he decided the time had come to leave Verrocchio and Florence. Leonardo would seek his destiny elsewhere.

North of Florence, the prosperous city of Milan boasted a brilliant university, musicians, architects, and fierce political intrigue. A cruel duke, Galeazzo Sforza, ruled the city until his murder in 1476. The duke's timid son, Gian, was heir to a vast fortune and title—but the eight-year-old was too young to assume power. When Gian was thirteen, his uncle, Ludovico Sforza, claimed guardianship of his nephew and took control of Milan, ruling the rich dukedom from a luxurious court.

Determined to make Milan the rival of any city in Europe, in particular Florence with its splendid reputation, Ludovico spent large sums of money to impress the powerful people he invited to his palace. Masquerades and glittering pageants, artists, magicians, jewels, even a suit of clothes spun of gold thread—Ludovico would spare no expense to bring glamour to Milan. Under his guidance, the city also became a center of trade and manufacturing. He organized experimental farming and introduced a new crop—rice. He built canals, roads, and schools. When he married, his wife, Beatrice d'Este, brought poets and scholars from all over Italy to entertain and enlighten her court.

The lute that Leonardo designed and gave to Ludovico was shaped like a horse's head, with ram's horns and a bird's beak, and was played upside down. Strings for the lute, played with a bow like a violin, stretched across the roof of the horse's mouth.

In 1482, when he was 30 years old, Leonardo leaped at the opportunity to go to Milan to deliver a gift for Ludovico from the Medicis of Florence—a beautiful silver lute, made by Leonardo himself. Leonardo realized that so rich and ambitious a man could be an excellent patron. Before he arrived, the artist wrote an amazing letter to Ludovico, boasting of his many talents. Leonardo promised that he could design bridges and build all kinds of new weapons, including improved cannons, warships, and "big guns." He also wrote that he could construct private and public buildings "to the equal of any other in architecture…" Near the end of a long list of accomplishments, Leonardo added, "I can carry out sculpture in marble and bronze, or clay, and also I can do in painting whatever may be done, as well as any other, be he who he may."

Despite Leonardo's many skills, Ludovico at first seemed most interested in using Leonardo's musical and artistic talents, as well as his quick wit, to amuse the lords and ladies of the court. The extravagant celebration of the wedding of Beatrice and Ludovico included banquets, theatrical performances, masquerade balls, and concerts. A group of artists worked on the entertainment. Leonardo designed costumes for actors dressed like "wild men" to frighten the ladies in attendance, and a great exhibition of fireworks blazed all night.

But Leonardo had more ambitious plans. Many knew that Ludovico wanted to erect a monument to honor his father, a legendary general, in the form of a fine bronze statue of the general astride his horse. Near the end of his extraordinary letter to Ludovico, Leonardo had written, "Moreover, the bronze horse could be made that will be to the immortal glory and eternal honor of the lord your father."

Ludovico's Mulberry Tree

Ludovico was called *Il Moro*. This may have been because of his dark complexion, or because the emblem of Ludovico was a mulberry tree, or both.

In Italian, the word *moro* can mean *Moor*, a person from Morocco or North Africa; or it can mean *dark-skinned* or *brown*. *Moro* is also the Italian word for *mulberry tree*.

After years of making sketches and proposals, Leonardo finally won the commission for a statue honoring General Sforza. The horse would stand at least twenty-four feet high—three or four times life-size—and be the most technically ambitious equestrian statue ever attempted. First it had to be formed out of clay; then, by pouring hot metal into molds made from this clay model, the horse would be cast in bronze.

Leonardo had worked on his ideas for this project on and off for more than ten years and finally succeeded in making a full-size clay model, which was exhibited with great fanfare in Milan in 1493. "Victory to the victor, and you, Vinci, have the victory!" sang the court poets in praise of him.

The triumphant Leonardo now turned to the daunting task of casting—the huge monument would require 80 tons of bronze. Ludovico had collected metal for the sculpture, but when war with France loomed in 1494, he decided art would have to wait. The bronze meant for the horse was melted down to make cannons. Eventually, victorious French soldiers entered Milan. Archers from the invading army used the colossal clay horse for target practice and destroyed it.

In 1490, Ludovico hosted the wedding of his nephew, the Duke Gian. For this celebration, Leonardo built the stage sets for a play, *"il paradiso"*—*paradise*. A hollow mountain opened to reveal a gilded view of the heavens. At the rim, torches glowed like stars, illuminating the signs of the zodiac. The stars were thought to influence destinies, and astrology was important. Actors representing the planets hung suspended from the ceiling and turned in orbit, eventually descending to pay compliments to the new bride. Ludovico's guests were astonished by the spectacle, and Leonardo's fame began to spread.

To design his statue, Leonardo studied stallions in the duke's stables, sketching them endlessly and learning even more about the horse through dissection. Then he made wax models, testing various positions for horse and rider. Originally he intended to show the animal rearing up and made hundreds of such drawings. Finally he realized the huge statue would be too heavy to stand on two legs, so he designed it to walk on three. His drawings are among the most beautiful and accurate studies of the horse ever produced.

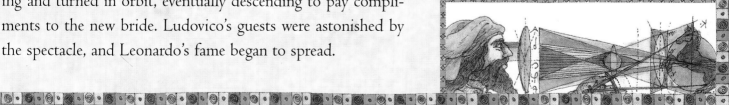

In 1495, while work on the horse was still under way, Ludovico asked Leonardo to paint one of the walls of a dining hall near a church called Santa Maria delle Grazie. The hall was part of a beautiful monastery in Milan, where monks lived bound together by religious vows. Their dining hall was the perfect setting for a powerful biblical scene that Leonardo had been thinking about, on and off, for fifteen years—the Last Supper. According to the Bible, on the night before he was crucified, Jesus shared a meal with his followers, blessing the bread and wine.

Leonardo thought it was important for a painter to show the feelings of his subjects, so he chose to illustrate a moment of great emotion during the supper. His painting explores how the twelve apostles reacted to the words "One of you shall betray me." From the energetic postures of their bodies, the gestures of their hands, and the expressions on their faces, we can see and feel the apostles' surprise, anger, horror, even guilt. Leonardo's ability to capture such enormous passion makes his version of a familiar scene breathtakingly original.

With skill and imagination, Leonardo used his mastery of perspective to make it almost seem as if the painting—fourteen feet high and thirty feet wide—is an extension of the dining room. The table, dishes, and glasses look like those the monks used. But in fact, the space created in the painting is on a higher, grander scale than the real space of the room. Leonardo's perspective also frames the figures in such a way that the eye of the viewer focuses directly on Christ, and the light through the window seems like his halo.

Some people consider the *Last Supper* to be the greatest of all of Leonardo's works. The painting made him famous throughout Europe during his lifetime, and over the last 500 years it has been endlessly studied and copied. Because of his experimental method of painting it and the ravages of time, the *Last Supper* has been the subject of many restorations and much controversy. The monastery is no longer used and the monks are gone, but this majestic work still looks hauntingly out of its space on the wall, one of the truly monumental works of art ever produced.

Painting on walls was usually done in a style called "fresco," using wet plaster and water-ba[sed] paint. This technique required the artist to w[ork] quickly. Leonardo liked to work slowly (it too[k] him three years to finish the *Last Supper*), so he experimented with tempera—an egg-based paint. First he coated the wall with varnish to protect his work from moisture. Unfortunate[ly,] the varnish reacted to acid and salt in the old wall itself. The results were disastrous: not long after the painting was completed, the tempera paint began to chip and flake off the wall. Fifty years later, almost nothing but cloudy shapes could be seen. The *Last Supper* has since been restored many times.

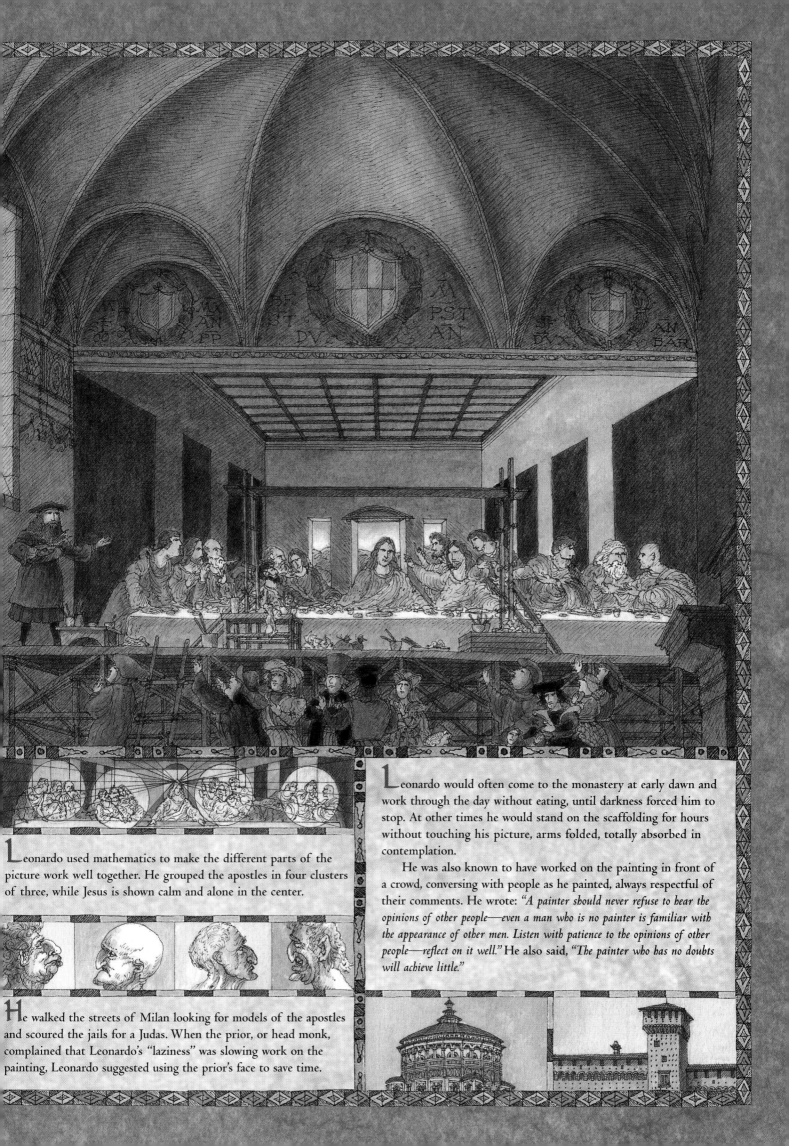

Leonardo used mathematics to make the different parts of the picture work well together. He grouped the apostles in four clusters of three, while Jesus is shown calm and alone in the center.

He walked the streets of Milan looking for models of the apostles and scoured the jails for a Judas. When the prior, or head monk, complained that Leonardo's "laziness" was slowing work on the painting, Leonardo suggested using the prior's face to save time.

Leonardo would often come to the monastery at early dawn and work through the day without eating, until darkness forced him to stop. At other times he would stand on the scaffolding for hours without touching his picture, arms folded, totally absorbed in contemplation.

He was also known to have worked on the painting in front of a crowd, conversing with people as he painted, always respectful of their comments. He wrote: *"A painter should never refuse to hear the opinions of other people—even a man who is no painter is familiar with the appearance of other men. Listen with patience to the opinions of other people—reflect on it well."* He also said, *"The painter who has no doubts will achieve little."*

Though Leonardo told tales of beasts and hunters, we know from his writings that he was a vegetarian strongly opposed to the killing of any creature for food or sport. *"Truly man is the king of beasts, for his brutality exceeds theirs. We live by the death of others: We are burial places!"* he wrote.

Ludovico must have been pleased with Leonardo's varied accomplishments and growing fame. After nine years in Milan, Leonardo was honored with the title of "ducal engineer." Although he had little money, the duke's new engineer enjoyed the comfort of his own workshop, with several servants and pupils to help him.

When he was not consumed by large projects, Leonardo spent much of his time working for Milan's aristocracy. He painted the portraits of several ladies and entertained members of the court with clever riddles and sensational tales. Stories of strange lands and even stranger animals were a favorite diver-

A favorite tale of Leonardo's was about the unicorn. According to legend, hunters could not catch this rare and elusive creature by themselves, but a lovesick unicorn would fall asleep on the lap of a beautiful maiden and then easily be trapped. Many people believed in unicorns and thought their horns had magical powers. The unicorn may be based on sightings of the rhinoceros, an African animal with one or two horns on its snout, or of the narwhal, an arctic whale with a long ivory tusk. Travelers and sailors returning from foreign lands sometimes exaggerated what they had seen.

sion. As wealthy as the nobles were, few among Leonardo's audience had ever ventured far from Italy. Travel was dangerous, and the lands that lay beyond Europe were considered mysterious and exotic. Anything seemed possible. Charming Leonardo proved to be a masterful storyteller. It is easy to imagine him regaling these naive aristocrats with enchanting tales of faraway places and fabulous beasts.

To what extent he was able to observe exotic animals or travel to foreign lands is unknown. In 1513, while working for Pope Leo X in Rome, Leonardo may have seen some unusual beasts in the Vatican zoo.

Leonardo said, "*Elephants have virtues rarely found in man: justice, honesty…they are merciful and compassionate.*" He also claimed, "*on account of their great weight they are unable to swim,*" and they eat stones. In fact, elephants don't eat stones, and they swim very well.

Leonardo admired the very organized world of bees. He observed, "*They live together in communities…some bees are ordered to go among the flowers, and others are ordered to work…others to take away the dirt, others to accompany and attend the king.*"

"*The bee,*" he notes, "*may be likened to deceit, for it has honey in its mouth and poison behind.*"

He dressed up a pet lizard like a monster to surprise and scare his friends.

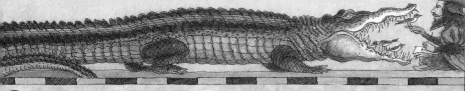

Of the crocodile, Leonardo said it lives in the river Nile, which is true, but he also claimed, "*it grows to a length of forty feet,*" which is an exaggeration. In his notebooks, he mentions a crocodile bird that walks among the great teeth, cleaning them. This seems amazing, but the Egyptian plover does pick insect parasites off of crocodiles.

He kept a pet porcupine and was greatly amused when its quills stuck dinner guests.

He wrote that the hippo has "*the teeth of a wild boar and a flowing mane.*" Of course hippos have no mane, but they are related to boars and have similar teeth.

Leonardo took great delight in inventing bizarre creatures. His "*Amphisbaena*" had two heads and could spit poison from both.

Leonardo explored phonetics, the study of sound and speech, to see if animals could learn to talk. "*Men will speak with animals of every kind, and they will answer in human speech,*" he predicted. He dissected a crocodile jaw and a woodpecker's tongue, comparing them to human jaws and tongues, to try to understand exactly how people are able to speak.

During his early years in Milan, Leonardo developed a system of writing his observations and ideas in small notebooks of linen paper, responding to everything and anything that caught the attention of his inquisitive mind. His notes and drawings originally filled over 13,000 pages on dozens of topics. Over half of these have been lost to us.

True to his restless nature, the notebooks show no order at all—Leonardo hoped to organize the pages later. Words and images are crammed together, wasting as little space as possible, since paper was precious. Drawings of anatomy lie side by side with maps and designs for cities. Remarks on what to eat for dinner occur on a page with geometry problems and plans for canals. In the privacy of these pages, Leonardo indulged daydreams, wry humor, even despair and loneliness in the face of

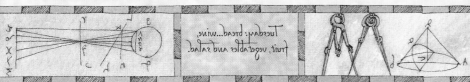

old age. Unless something was intended for others, Leonardo wrote backward, from right to left. This reversed script reads easily only when it is held up to a mirror. Why did he do this? No one is sure. Perhaps he wanted to keep his work secret. He hoped to publish his notes someday, and this way of writing would make his ideas hard to steal. He also knew that the Church thought some of his notions were dangerous. Perhaps it simply felt natural because he was left-handed. By writing from right to left, it was easier to avoid ink smudges. Or he may have used "mirror writing" for his own amusement—he loved anything bizarre or unusual.

Leonardo tried to understand exactly how things worked, asking himself questions that had never been asked before. His notebooks combine thoughts on the forces of nature and practical science with the power and grace of his art. They offer a fascinating glimpse into the unguarded dreams of a genius.

"This is to be a collection without order, taken from many papers... I shall have to repeat the same thing many times... because the subjects are many, and memory cannot contain them."

The ancient Romans realized that with mathematically precise construction, the semicircular form of an arch could support a great deal of weight. Leonardo made many studies of arches, trying to improve their strength. *"An arch is nothing other than a strength built on two weaknesses,"* he wrote. In his notes he explains that an arch is made of two quarter circles, which by themselves are weak. But fitted together at the top of a window or door, the semicircle becomes strong. Together, *"the two weaknesses are converted into a single strength."*

Leonardo learned the principles of architecture—how to design sturdy, beautiful buildings—by studying Roman ruins and the works of Renaissance architects. As an apprentice in Verrocchio's studio, he had been impressed and inspired by the construction of Brunelleschi's great dome for the cathedral of Florence. The circle was Leonardo's favorite shape, and his best-known designs feature a large dome surrounded by many smaller ones.

In Milan, he worked with the innovative architect Bramante, who designed churches for Ludovico and later for Pope Julius.

Leonardo gave useful advice for the ongoing construction of Milan's cathedral, a complicated project that was over a century old and the subject of much debate when he arrived. (In his opinion, the building was "sick" and needed an architect who could be its doctor.) He even entered a competition to design the cathedral's dome.

In 1485, the plague killed as many as one in three people in Milan. Leonardo blamed the disaster on crowded, dirty living conditions, and he set about designing an ideal city. His plans called for channels of water to carry off refuse "so that the air of the city may not be polluted." He sketched wide streets to supply fresh air and sun, with an elevated level for pedestrians. He designed staircases between the levels, paying careful attention to the flow of people through the city.

Leonardo seems to have been more interested in his innovative architectural ideas than in the practicalities of construction, however. Most of his grand plans were never realized.

While studying the Duke of Milan's horses for the great statue of the duke's father, Leonardo drew up plans for a model stable with all sorts of innovations—pumps to fill the troughs with water, wall channels to automatically refill mangers with fodder, and underground tunnels to remove manure. Twenty-five years later, Leonardo's plans were used to build the Medicis' new stables in Florence, accommodating 128 horses. The only one of his architectural designs to be built, Leonardo's stables still stand. The building now houses the *Istituto Geografico Militare* (the Italian Military Geographic Institute).

Leonardo thought that enemy cannon-balls would bounce off this fort he designed with round walls. Each wall was protected by a moat.

Leonardo designed a bridge for the Sultan of Turkey that was to be over 1,000 feet long and *"so high that tall masted ships could sail under it."*

After the outbreak of the plague, Ludovico sought out architectural projects and monuments to make his capital ever more beautiful and impressive. Leonardo obliged with designs for towers, fountains, churches, and his plans for an ideal city. He also considered ways to improve the safety of buildings. Studies of fissures in walls and the effects of earthquakes on foundations exist in his notes. He investigated the strength of different materials and how to make structures strong.

The span of a man's outspread arms is equal to his height.

Vitruvius, a Roman architect, believed a man with outstretched arms and legs would fit perfectly into a square and circle. Many Renaissance scholars accepted this was so, but attempts to draw such a man always produced obvious distortions. As a result of his studies, Leonardo was able to correct Vitruvius's measurements and offer more accurate proportions. *"With what words, O writer, can you with a like perfection describe [this] as does the drawing?"*

Compare the legs of a frog to those of a man: They have great resemblance.

How do we walk? How do bones and muscles move? Leonardo visited hospitals, observing doctors at work. In 1503, when his new workshop was in the Santa Maria Novella hospital in Florence, he watched doctors operate; at night he dissected bodies, often the corpses of criminals. Though the Church frowned on dissection, toward the end of his life Leonardo boasted to the Cardinal of Aragon of his gruesome, groundbreaking work. *"[I have] dissected the corpses of more than thirty men and women of all ages."*

Leonardo's interest in anatomy probably began in Verrocchio's workshop. Most artists of his time learned only enough about skeletons and muscles to allow them to strive for beauty and naturalness in their paintings and sculpture. But to Leonardo the body posed fascinating mysteries.

In Milan he began dissecting corpses, searching for clues to how the body works. He believed that drawing the body was the most complete way to understand it. He drew organs, joints, bones, tissues from many angles, including cross sections, revealing the relationship between form and function with a beauty and clarity never before seen. Until Leonardo, teachers of anatomy thought pictures would confuse students. But in

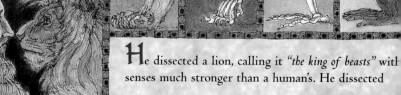

He dissected a lion, calling it *"the king of beasts"* with senses much stronger than a human's. He dissected

1543, the first modern medical textbook, *De Humanis Corporis Fabrica*, included illustrations inspired by his drawings. Similar pictures are still used today to teach anatomy. His sketch *The Vitruvian Man* shows his understanding of anatomy and proportion; it may be the best known of all his drawings.

Leonardo also dissected animals, including bears, monkeys, cows, and frogs. In botany, he was the first to make detailed drawings of plants. Always searching out the essential connections between living things, he compared their leaves and stems to human anatomy. He likened the circulation of blood to the flow of rivers and the pulsing of the heart to the rhythm of ocean tides. "Man is the model of the universe," he said.

"*What moves you, O man…if it is not the beauty of the natural world?*" Leonardo's respect for nature guided all of his work. He compared the branches of a tree to the veins in our bodies as he studied circulation. He discovered a tree's age by counting the rings in its trunk. He believed artists should paint plants and trees as carefully as they study and paint people. This viewpoint was not shared by many artists of his time, but Leonardo counseled, "*Consult nature in everything.*"

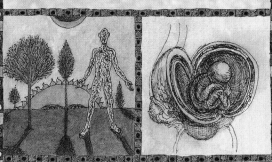

At times in his sketches, Leonardo relied upon similarities between animals and humans. One of his drawings of a human baby in the womb is remarkably correct except for the placenta, or sac, surrounding the baby. Scientists today think the shape of the sac in Leonardo's drawing is actually based on the placenta of a cow.

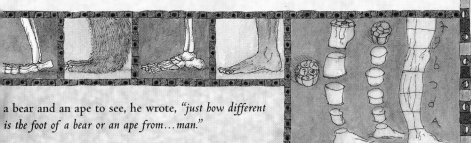

a bear and an ape to see, he wrote, "*just how different is the foot of a bear or an ape from…man.*"

"Now do you not see that the eye embraces the beauty of the whole world?"

"It has measured the distance and sizes of the stars."

"The eye is the window of the soul."

LEONARDO'S
SCHEMATIC EYE

Leonardo invented a simple projector. Inside a box, candlelight reaches a flower and then passes through a glass lens in the side of the box. The lens focuses and projects the light onto a flat surface, where the image of the flower appears.

His *camera obscura* worked like a camera. He wrote: *"...when the species of illuminated objects penetrate into a very dark chamber by some small round hole. Then you will receive these species on a white paper within this dark room and rather near to the hole, and you will see all the objects on paper in their proper forms and colors, but much smaller; and they will be upside down by reason of that very intersection. These images, being transmitted from a place illuminated by the sun, still seem actually painted on this paper."*

Who would believe that so small a space could contain the images of all the universe?" Given his skill at observing and his talent as a visual artist, it is only natural that Leonardo would be fascinated by the wonder and power of the human eye. "It has discovered the elements...and given birth to the divine art of painting," he wrote. For Leonardo, the eye was the most remarkable organ in the body, a thing "superior to all others created by God." It gave humans a "most complete and magnificent view of the infinite works of nature."

In order to investigate the mystery of eyesight for himself, Leonardo once again turned to examination and dissection. The eye is soft, but he discovered that by boiling the organ with egg white, he could make it firm enough to dissect. He also tried to imitate the workings of the eye and its parts by building a model with glass instruments.

Of the five senses, he said: *"This is the eye, the chief and leader of all others."*

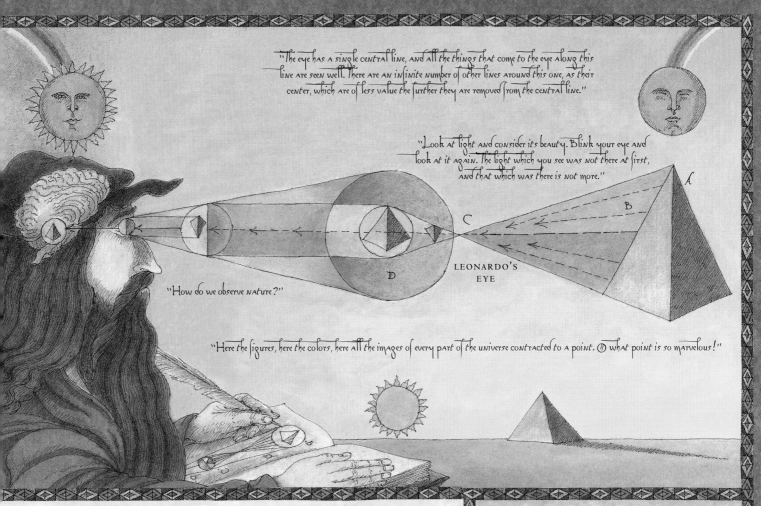

"The eye has a single central line, and all the things that come to the eye along this line are seen well. There are an infinite number of other lines around this one, as their center, which are of less value the further they are removed from the central line."

"Look at light and consider its beauty. Blink your eye and look at it again. The light which you see was not there at first, and that which was there is not more."

A

B

C

LEONARDO'S
EYE

D

"How do we observe nature?"

"Here the figures, here the colors, here all the images of every part of the universe contracted to a point. O what point is so marvelous!"

The ancient Greeks believed that the eye sent forth sight rays, and when the rays hit objects, we were able to see them. Leonardo realized that their theory was wrong: "It is impossible that the eye should project the visual power from itself," he wrote. He understood that if sight rays came from the eye, it would take time for the rays to reach an object. He pointed out that we see objects instantly, as soon as we open our eyes, and he used the sun as a counterexample to the Greek theory. Although the sun is a great distance from us, as soon as we look at it we see it. If rays came from the eye, he reasoned, it would take a long time to see the sun. He thought perhaps "a month." The theory of vision Leonardo worked out came very close to realizing how the eye actually works. "No Image, even of the smallest object, enters the eye without being turned upside down," he wrote.

HIS THEORY OF VISION

Leonardo reasoned that we see an object, *A*, because light, *B*, reflected off that object passes through a small opening in the surface of the eye, *C*, becoming inverted, and then reaches a lens, *D*, in the center of the eye, which turns it right side up. He didn't know, as we do now, that the optic nerve carries the upside-down image to the brain, which rights it.

"*All things in the cosmos travel in waves.*" He guessed the sun was 4,000 miles away. It is 93 million.

Leonardo studied the pupil of the eye, which dilates, or grows large, in darkness, and contracts, becoming smaller, when it receives light. "*Cats, screech owls, long-eared owls…have the pupil small at mid-day and very large at night,*" he observed. He also worked out the causes of farsightedness and designed his own spectacles. He even envisioned how a lens contacting the eye directly could one day correct eyesight.

eonardo saw in the body and its parts, including the eye, a beautiful, complicated machine. As an engineer in Ludovico's court, and in his own notebooks, Leonardo had the opportunity to turn his inventive genius to the wonderful potential of man-made machines.

Much of the power during Leonardo's time was supplied simply by the muscles of people and animals. Animals pulled wagons, turned millstones, dragged plows; people cut grain, thatched roofs, laid bricks, built scaffolding, chiseled stone. Leonardo pondered ways to harness forces such as wind, steam, and moving water to help people accomplish their tasks in less time, with less work, and with more spectacular results. Inspired by the potential of technology, he wrote of humankind: "With a little power they can move and raise the greatest weights, outwitting nature with their machines."

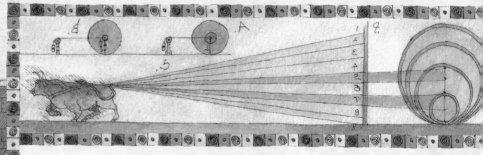

Leonardo drew a spindle that wound thread in a method similar to that used in factories today. He studied different types of screws, pulleys, and axles, and his notebooks show the uses he made of them for scores of helpful devices. Sometimes he put his mind to the task of destruction. When he later worked for eight months as engineer-in-chief to Cesare Borgia, a ruthless warlord, Leonardo designed weapons, drew maps, and made suggestions for improvements to Borgia's fortresses.

eonardo's movable crane, balanced with a guide wire at the top, was mounted on a cart and could revolve on a pivot. The crane was meant to lift stone blocks up to the workers. A crank turned a small gear, which turned a larger gear. This turned an axle, and the rope pulled up the load of building blocks. The gears provided most of the power. The pivot that allowed the crane to turn was at the bottom.

One of Leonardo's most surprising designs was for a bicycle, a more elegant one than the first modern bicycles produced 300 years later. Leonardo's design called for a chain, exactly like today's bikes.

Most of Leonardo's inventions were never built, possibly because the construction techniques of the Renaissance were not equal to his grand designs, or because his patrons lacked money and interest. Perhaps his reluctance to share his ideas played a role, or his own disinterest in seeing his projects through to their practical conclusions. Modern scholars, however, have produced working models of many of his designs.

"*Nothing is moved, unless it is moved upon.*" Leonardo proved that no lifeless object can move by itself. It needs to be moved by some other force. For a long time this theory was called Leonardo's Law. Today we call it Newton's First Law of Motion, or the Law of Inertia. The principle was worked out in a mathematical formula by Sir Isaac Newton in the 17th century.

Hours   Minutes

PISTON

CLOCK

Steam
Water

Heat

Leonardo invented a clock with two faces, one that showed hours and one that showed minutes. Before this, clocks displayed hours only. Two separate clockworks were moved by weights on cords wound around cylinders. These turned wheels that turned gears attached to the hands. Leonardo's revolutionary idea for a steam-powered piston predates the development of the first steam engine by 150 years.

Among Leonardo's plans were a mechanical drum, a monkey wrench, and a horseless wagon that moved by springs and pulleys tied to wheels, like a child's windup toy.

THE ETERNAL BIRDMAN

For 25 years, one idea tantalized Leonardo above all others: that human beings might actually fly. He made hundreds of drawings for flying machines, taking inspiration from nature's work. He watched leaves falling, noting their slow descent. He saw that the wings of bats acted like sails, allowing the creatures to float and glide. He made drawings of bats and birds and came to understand how air currents keep them aloft just as water keeps a swimmer afloat. Most of Leonardo's designs for flying machines were based on his studies of birds' flapping wings, but he was never able to solve the problem of how to generate enough power to get a machine off the ground and airborne. We now know that his machines were far too heavy to achieve liftoff through the power of human arms and legs moving artificial wings.

Leonardo locked himself in his rooms and built large models of some of his designs in secret. He called his flying gadgets *uccello,* Italian for *bird.* It is believed he may have tested at least one, a model held together by an oxhide thong, for he wrote in his notebook: "Tomorrow morning on the second day of January, 1496, I will make the thong and the attempt." But there is no further mention of it. Did he ever actually see the world from *"una vista d'uccello,"* his wishful bird's-eye view?

In 1505, studies of flight and schemes for flying machines mysteriously come to an end in Leonardo's notes. Did he become disillusioned with his dream of flying, or was he distracted by a passion for some new project?

"If a man have a tent of closely woven linen without any apertures, twelve braccia across and twelve braccia in depth, he can throw himself down from any great height without injury."
(*braccia* is Italian for *arm*)

As far as we know, Leonardo's last written words about flying were: *"From Monte Ceceri the famous bird will take its flight, which will fill the world with its great renown."*

Modern studies of a 15th-century French painting and a 16th-century stained-glass window show children playing with a toy that had wooden propellerlike blade on top of a centra revolving spindle. When a cord attached to the spindle was pulled and quickly released, centripetal force revolved the propeller one way an then the other. It seems likely that Leonardo's helicopter was partly inspired by a child's toy.

Leonardo's helicopter was basically a rotatin screw, which he called a "helix," Greek for *spira.*

"See how the wings striking against the air hold up the heavy eagle in the thin upper air, near to the element of fire. And likewise see how the air moving over the sea strikes against the bellying sails, making the loaded heavy ship run, so that by these demonstrative and definite reasons you may know that man with his great contrived wings, battling the resistant air and conquering it, can subject it and rise above it."

"A bird is an instrument working according to mathematical law."

"As much pressure is exerted by the object against the air as by the air against the body."

"Dissect the bat, study it carefully, and on this model construct the machine."

"Remember that your bird should have no other model than the bat."

Leonardo knew that water evaporated from the sea and returned to earth as rain, traveling by rivers and streams to the oceans again. His theory of wave motion, 150 years before it was proved: *"Nothing is carried away from the shore by the waves of the sea. The sea casts back to the shore all things left at sea. The surface of the water keeps the imprint of the water for some time."*

Water held a lifelong attraction for Leonardo. He believed it was the driving force of nature. By understanding the laws of water's movement through the air and earth, in rain, rivers, and streams, he hoped to better understand all creation. Thoughts about the nature of water and about machines to utilize its power run throughout his notebooks. Leonardo sketched water rising, splashing, churning, and moving in waves. His eye and hand were so quick that, until photography, his drawings were the most accurate images of water ever seen. But Leonardo also feared water's destructive power. As an old man, he made frightening drawings of a great deluge, sweeping away civilization and ending the world.

THE FOUR ELEMENTS

Leonardo, along with other scholars of his time, believed the ancient Greek theory that the world is made up of four elements: earth, air, fire, and water. To him, water was by far the most important of these. He believed that the human body was also made up of the four elements and was a miniature universe. Our blood acts like the tides of the ocean, he thought, rising and falling every six hours. He felt that people and the earth function in similar ways and wrote that we breathe *"with the breathing of the world."*

THE FOUR COLORS

Leonardo believed painting should imitate nature and that the four elements were related to color: fire was red, air blue, water green, and earth yellow.

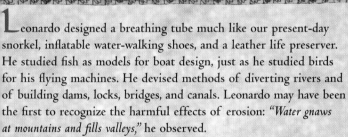

Leonardo designed a breathing tube much like our present-day snorkel, inflatable water-walking shoes, and a leather life preserver. He studied fish as models for boat design, just as he studied birds for his flying machines. He devised methods of diverting rivers and of building dams, locks, bridges, and canals. Leonardo may have been the first to recognize the harmful effects of erosion: *"Water gnaws at mountains and fills valleys,"* he observed.

Leonardo realized that the sky itself is not blue. *"I say that the blue which is seen in the atmosphere is not its own color."* He thought that the sun's rays strike tiny particles of moisture in the air, causing bright blue light to reflect against the dark atmosphere above. Scientists today speak about the selective scattering of the blue wavelength of light as it strikes dust, water vapor, and other particles in the air.

When a monk named Luca Pacioli was invited to Milan to teach mathematics in 1496, Leonardo quickly found in him a guide and inspiration in the field of mathematics. Pacioli, in turn, was fascinated by Leonardo's many theories, mechanical ideas, and inventions. Leonardo provided the illustrations for Pacioli's book on geometry, *De Divina proportione.*

In Leonardo's time, our view of the moon, planets, sun, and stars was called "The Vault of Heaven." Most scholars believed that the earth was at its center, surrounded by other celestial bodies. Based on his own studies, Leonardo rejected this. He theorized that the sun was the center of the universe. "The sun does not move," he wrote. "In the universe there is no greater magnitude and power than the sun."

He became fascinated with the idea of a universal truth, wondering if some mighty force could connect humans, animals, plants, earth, and water. He came to believe that the study of mathematics would provide proof of a perfect balance in all creation. Some scholars suspected the existence of

"*Although the stars appear small, many are of a size larger than earth.*" He called the earth "*this star of ours.*"

A total eclipse of the sun was seen from Milan, March 26, 1485. Leonardo devised a "*method of seeing the sun eclipsed without pain to the eye. Take a piece of paper and pierce holes in it with a needle, and look at the sun through these holes.*"

universal mathematical laws providing order for the entire universe. Ratios, or the numerical comparison of one thing to another, could be used to organize and understand everything from harmonies in music to the movement of the planets. Knowing how proportions and geometry work in the natural world, Leonardo thought, was the key to understanding a universal truth. "There is no certainty in sciences where one of the mathematical sciences cannot be applied, or which are not in relation with mathematics," he wrote. In the chaos of the Renaissance world—amidst wars, floods, and disasters like the plague—the idea of a rational order guiding the natural world may have given Leonardo great comfort.

Did Leonardo have plans to build some kind of telescope? Over 100 years before Galileo turned a telescope on the heavens, Leonardo had written in his notebook: *"Make glasses in order to see the moon large."* His design for a telescope had two lenses, one convex and one concave. The convex lens was already used for magnifying, but the addition of the concave lens, *"thick in the edges, thin in the middle,"* was new.

Leonardo disputed the view of the ancient Greeks that the moon and the planets produce their own light. He wrote, *"The moon has no light of itself. It does not shine without the sun. The moon acts like a spherical mirror."*

"Every part of the whole must be in proportion to the whole...applying to all animals and plants."

"Paint the face in such a way that it will be easy to understand what is going on in the mind."

While painting, Leonardo often had musicians, singers, and entertainers perform to create a festive mood.

Leonardo gave this advice to students: "*In the streets when night is falling, in bad weather, observe what delicacy and grace appear in the faces of men and women…You may paint your picture at the end of the day, when there are clouds or mist, and this atmosphere is perfect…to this is added the grace of the shadows, which have no harsh contours but blend harmoniously into one another.*" He himself spent years learning to achieve the illusion of a silken haziness, or "no harsh contours," by painting layers of thin oil glazes on top of each other.

When French troops forced Duke Ludovico to flee Milan, Leonardo found himself once again in search of a patron. He set out for Venice with his friend the mathematician Luca Pacioli and worked as a military engineer for the Venetian Senate and later for the warlord Cesare Borgia.

In 1503 Leonardo returned to Florence and began a portrait that he never titled—it became known as *La Gioconda* in Italian and the *Mona Lisa* in English. Although the face in the painting is now famous, no one knows for certain who the woman was. Most scholars believe Leonardo received a commission from a wealthy Florentine silk merchant and that the woman is his wife, Lisa del Giocondo. Leonardo would labor over the painting for many years, bringing to

Leonardo believed that in painting, landscape was more important than just a background for the human figure. He envisioned people and nature together in a natural environment. *"He is not well rounded who does not have an equally keen interest in all of the things within the compass of painting."*

As Leonardo worked on the *Mona Lisa*, he also began to paint a scene from Florence's history—*The Battle of Anghiari*—for a new council hall. In Leonardo's design, there is no setting, and the warriors' costumes suggest no particular time period. All of the elements of his composition—the men's enraged faces, their swords, and the horses' bodies—curve inward; there is no escape from deadly combat. Leonardo hated war, calling it *pazzia bestialissima*—*"most beastly madness."* His rival, Michelangelo, was also asked to paint a scene. The two men did not like each other. Michelangelo was quarrelsome and insulted Leonardo for never finishing his great horse. Leonardo called Michelangelo's muscular sculptures *"bags of nuts"* and considered sculpture inferior to painting: "[Sculpture is] *a wholly mechanical exercise that is often accompanied by much sweat…the painter sits at great ease in front of his work, well dressed…*" Leonardo tried not to quarrel with Michelangelo in public. *"He who does not control his impulses classes himself with the beasts."* Although they both made large cartoons, or life-size sketches, neither artist ever finished his painting.

bear all his powers of observation and technical skill.

For centuries, people have marveled over the *Mona Lisa*'s glowing flesh, her mysterious expression, and the delicate details of her dress and of the landscape behind her. Leonardo achieves a sensual realism by making it seem the woman is emerging from darkness, not a figure painted onto a white surface. The palpable feel of hazy atmosphere comes from his mastery of *sfumato*—his ability to paint shadows as subtle as smoke. The figure in the portrait is closer to the viewer than was traditional, giving the *Mona Lisa* an impressive intimacy.

A young painter named Raphael copied the *Mona Lisa* before it was finished and adopted its innovations in his own popular works. Leonardo had changed portraiture forever.

This is a clock for the use of those who watch jealously over the use of their time.

"O thou that sleepest, what is sleep? Sleep is an image of death....Do not let yourself sleep at midday."

Many of Leonardo's experiments were not appreciated by others. He once made bizarre creatures out of soft wax and filled them with air. Then he released the grotesque beasts in the Vatican gardens, surprising and terrifying visitors. His practical joke may have looked silly, but Leonardo had a purpose: to see how air expands when heated and how it could be useful. Did he dream of flying vessels like our modern hot-air balloons? In Rome, Leonardo's study of human anatomy continued, though it, too, was controversial—he was denied permission to dissect bodies at the Hospital of the Holy Spirit. His advice and maps did prove useful when his patron, Giuliano, set out to drain dangerous marshes south of the city.

In 1513, having spent a number of years working for the French conquerors of Milan, the aging Leonardo was invited to come under the patronage of Giuliano de' Medici, commander of the papal troops and brother of the newly appointed Pope Leo X. Leonardo traveled to Rome, bringing with him thousands of pages of notes, various paintings and instruments, his faithful friend and student Francesco Melzi, and a precocious young servant Leonardo called "Salai," or *demon*.

Pope Leo, known for his love of humor, surrounded himself with jesters and odd, amusing characters. Leonardo, a famed practical joker, found ways to please him. A favorite trick of

Leonardo's was to fix a sheep's intestine onto a large bellows. Hiding out of sight, he would pump the bellows, inflating the thin, expandable intestine until it filled the room like a giant balloon and flattened people against the walls.

Leonardo considered extra sleep wasteful, so he invented an alarm clock. All night, water dripped into a bucket suspended in midair and attached to a tube. As the drips accumulated, the bucket lowered; by morning it was low enough to cause a pan on the other end of the tube to dump its water into the bucket also. The bucket plunged downward from the sudden extra weight, jerking the sleeper's feet upward with an awakening jolt.

Leonardo found Rome full of competition, and his notes at this time admit discouragement. Young Raphael was famous and the pope's favorite painter. An old rival, Michelangelo, had just completed a series of magnificent frescoes for the pope's Sistine Chapel. Leonardo, on the other hand, was never fully accepted by the papal court. When asked to do a small painting, he decided to first work on a varnish for the picture. The pope cried, "This man will never accomplish anything! He thinks of the end before the beginning." There were no more papal commissions for Leonardo.

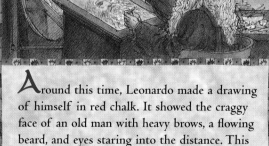

Around this time, Leonardo made a drawing of himself in red chalk. It showed the craggy face of an old man with heavy brows, a flowing beard, and eyes staring into the distance. This striking self-portrait is usually thought to be our only accurate likeness of him.

THE PERFECT PATRON

King Louis XII, the father-in-law of Francis I, liked Leonardo's *Last Supper* so much that he proposed moving the dining-hall wall to France. Later, Francis would share this esteem for Leonardo. The artist's chateau was connected to the palace by an underground tunnel. Francis could visit Leonardo as often as he wished.

Leonardo remained in the service of the pope's brother, Giuliano de' Medici, until Giuliano died in 1516. Then the old master traveled to France at the invitation of the young French king, Francis I. A year earlier, Leonardo had presented Francis with a mechanical lion that could walk a few steps by means of springs and levers. When the king tapped the lion on the nose, its chest opened to reveal a great bouquet of lilies, the flower of France. The unusual gift intrigued Francis.

The king was a bold, intelligent ruler and a generous patron of art, literature, and learning. He installed Leonardo in a

chateau near the royal court at Amboise and honored him as the "Premier Painter, Engineer, and Architect to the King." In return he asked Leonardo to teach him about art and nature.

Accompanied by Melzi and Salai, Leonardo arrived in France with his library, notebooks, and a few paintings, including the *Mona Lisa*. Francis tried to buy it many times, but Leonardo would never sell. On his master's death, Salai inherited the paintings. Twelve years later, in 1530, the king finally had his chance to purchase the coveted portrait. That is why it hangs today in Paris, France, and not in Italy.

Of Leonardo, Francis I said he did not believe "…that any other mind had ever been born into the world who knew so much as Leonardo, not only in sculpture, painting, and architecture, but still more in that he was a very great philosopher." According to legend, Leonardo died in the arms of the king.

"I *have wasted my hours....Tell me if anything at all was done.*"

Francesco Melzi was born to an aristocratic family in the town of Vaprio, near Milan. Around 1507, at age 15, he met Leonardo and soon after left his family to become an apprentice and assistant to the master—an unusual choice of career for a well-to-do young nobleman. Melzi was devastated by the death of his great friend and teacher. "For so long as my limbs endure, I shall possess a perpetual sorrow," he wrote. "It is a hurt to anyone to lose such a man, for nature cannot again produce his like."

As a well spent day brings sleep," Leonardo wrote, "so a life well lived brings a happy death." But as he grew older, Leonardo questioned the value of his life's work. Most of his thousands of plans and projects were unfinished. His notes remained unpublished, and so the range and depth of his inquiries were known just to close friends. Though a celebrated artist, he had completed only a few paintings, and several already showed damage. Had he achieved anything worthwhile?

On May 2, 1519, after suffering a partial paralysis in his last years, Leonardo died at the age of 67. He was buried in accordance with his wishes, in the Church of St. Florentine in Amboise, France. Francesco Melzi, his loyal friend and pupil, inherited Leonardo's precious notebooks. He kept what he called "the infinite number of volumes" more than 50 years and organized the notes on painting into a collection called the *Treatise on Painting.* It was eventually published and widely circu-

lated. As a result, for centuries to come Leonardo would be famous primarily as an artist.

Unfortunately, Melzi's heirs did not understand the significance of Leonardo's papers. When Melzi died, his family allowed treasure hunters and collectors to carry off pieces of the notebooks, and the pages were soon scattered haphazardly across Europe. Over half of the work was destroyed or lost.

During the Industrial Revolution, inventions in science and engineering suddenly seemed to chart the future. Leonardo's mechanical designs and studies of the natural world inspired new interest and respect. In the 1880s, portions of his notes devoted to many fields of science were published for the first time. The marvelously strange style of his notebooks and his dazzling artistic talent, imbued with mystery by such a lack of published or finished work, ensured that Leonardo would be one of the most compelling figures in all of history.

The house where Leonardo spent his final years still stands. The personal belongings he took to Amboise were few, considering his productive life. He had his immense collection of drawings and notes; his books, including a Bible, Pliny's *Natural History*, Plutarch's *Lives*, Euclid's study of geometry, and countryman Alberti's *Treatise on Architecture*; and just three paintings: the *St. Anne*, the *St. John*, and the *Mona Lisa*. An entry in the church register still reads: "In the cloister of this church was buried M. Leonardo da Vinci, a nobleman from Milan, engineer and architect to the King, state master of mechanics and one-time Director of Painting to the Duke of Milan."

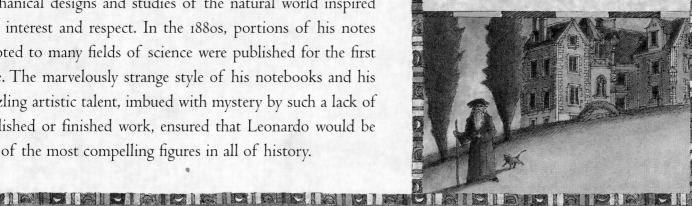

Truly marvelous and celestial was Leonardo.

—THE LIVES OF THE ARTISTS

by Giorgio Vasari, 16th-century biographer

Shortly after Leonardo da Vinci's death, a scholar named Vasari wrote a series of biographies vividly describing events in the lives of many important artists of the Renaissance, including Leonardo. Vasari pieced together scraps of evidence from Leonardo's life with tales told by those who knew him, in order to create a colorful, impressive—though not always reliable—written portrait.

Since Vasari, writers and scholars from many fields have reinterpreted Leonardo's life and work, struggling to create a compelling account of this enigmatic man and his continuing importance. Renaissance troubadours sang of his fame; modern poets such as Oscar Wilde and William Butler Yeats also wrote about him. In 1910, the psychologist Sigmund Freud turned his analytical skills to Leonardo and published *Leonardo da Vinci and a Memory of His Childhood.* Einstein would ponder the merits of Leonardo's science. Artists and critics from the 16th century's Raphael to modern pop-art creator Andy Warhol have felt Leonardo's influence. Each generation seems to seize upon his work in a new way.

Modern research and lucky discoveries uncovering lost documents and artwork have shed new light on the past. Still, historians continue to argue about the dates and details of Leonardo's life and art. Questions regarding his commissions, his subjects, or how much of a picture he actually painted himself have led to controversy and debate.

Today's scholars, like those who have come before, delight in discovering and reinventing Leonardo. But we can all think of him as a supremely gifted artist and a revolutionary inquirer. His work and his dreams, preserved in museums and in his fabulous notebooks, can be trusted to take all who discover them on a journey from the ancient to the modern world, and perhaps to worlds we don't yet know.

TIMELINE

The "c" that precedes some dates means "circa" ("approximately").

April 24, 1452 Birth of Leonardo near Vinci, in Tuscany, Italy

1456 A powerful hurricane devastates Tuscany—the source of Leonardo's fascination with the power of water?

c1468 Leonardo enters Verrocchio's workshop in Florence.

1469 Birth of Machiavelli, author of *The Prince,* about gaining and holding political power

1471 Brunelleschi's sphere and cross crown the magnificent dome of Florence's cathedral. Verrocchio's workshop is responsible for casting the two-ton sculpture and devising a method to lift it into place.

1473 Date of Leonardo's first known work, *Landscape Drawing of the Arno Valley,* now in the Galleria degli Uffizi, in Florence

1473 Birth of Copernicus, a Polish astronomer, who will study the heavens and claim that the Earth rotates around the sun

1473 Leonardo admitted to the painters' guild, in Florence

c1473–1476 The *Annunciation* is completed. This painting is now in the Uffizi in Florence. Leonardo assists Verrocchio on a painting called The *Baptism of Christ* (Uffizi, Florence).

1475 Birth of Michelangelo, who will become Leonardo's great rival

c1475–1478 Leonardo paints *Portrait of Ginevra de' Benci,* now in the National Gallery of Art in Washington, D.C.

c1478 Leonardo paints *Madonna and Child* (also known as *Madonna with a Flower* or *Benois Madonna*), a portrait of Mary and the baby Jesus, now displayed in the Hermitage, in St. Petersburg, Russia.

1480 Birth of Magellan, a Portuguese sea captain. In 1519, just after Leonardo's death, he will be the first man to circumnavigate the globe.

1481 Leonardo is commissioned to paint the *Adoration of the Magi,* a Bible scene. Though unfinished, the *Adoration* is considered a masterpiece. It hangs today in the Uffizi, in Florence.

c1482 Leonardo moves to Milan and becomes part of Ludovico's court. About this time, he begins to keep his notebooks.

1483 Birth of Raphael, a brilliant painter and architect, considered with Leonardo and Michelangelo to be one of the three greatest artists of the period known as the High Renaissance

c1483–1486 Leonardo, assisted by two lesser artists, paints the *Virgin of the Rocks,* now in the Louvre, in Paris.

1485 A total eclipse of the sun, which Leonardo may have observed

c1484–1486 A plague in Milan inspires Leonardo's plans for an ideal city.

1487–1488 Leonardo participates in a design competition for the dome of Milan's cathedral and consults in the Milan Cathedral Workshop.

c1488 Leonardo makes sketches for his great horse and studies anatomy.

c1490 Leonardo establishes his own workshop in Milan.

January 1490 Leonardo's *Il Paradiso* provides dazzling entertainment for the marriage celebrations of young duke Gian Galeazzo Sforza, Ludovico's nephew, to Isabella of Aragon in Milan.

1490 Leonardo begins notes for a treatise on water power, or hydraulics.

July 1490 Giacomo, a precocious 10-year-old boy, comes to live with Leonardo as a servant. He proves to be a lovable pest, stealing money and taking a silverpoint pencil from one of Leonardo's pupils. Leonardo nicknames him *Salai*—Tuscan for "demon." Salai will continue to annoy his master, but Leonardo grows very fond of him and invites him everywhere. Giacomo will stay with Leonardo until his master's death in 1519.

1491 Leonardo designs costumes for the fantastic celebrations surrounding the double wedding of Ludovico with Beatrice d'Este and Anna Sforza (Ludovico's niece) with Alfonso d'Este.

1492 Christopher Columbus, an Italian, sails west from Europe to what will be called the New World. He believes he has reached Asia.

c1488–1493 Leonardo paints portraits of members of the Milanese court, including Ludovico's mistress, Cecilia Gallerani, in *Lady with the Ermine.*

1493 A clay model of Leonardo's horse is displayed with great festivity in Milan. Those who see it consider the horse a wonder.

1494 Ludovico Sforza officially becomes Duke of Milan when his nephew dies.

early 1490s Leonardo observes birds to develop a theory of flight and sketches designs for many flying machines.

c1495–1496 Leonardo may have attempted flight in a flying contraption.

1495–1498 Leonardo paints the *Last Supper.*

1496 Luca Pacioli, Franciscan monk and mathematician, arrives in Milan. Leonardo becomes his friend and is newly fascinated by mathematics.

c1499 Leonardo draws a cartoon, or life-size sketch, for the *Virgin and Child with St. Anne and the Young St. John the Baptist.* It is now in the National Gallery, London.

1499 The French invade Milan and destroy Leonardo's horse.

1499–1500 Leonardo sets out for Venice and works for the Venetian Senate as a military engineer.

1502 Leonardo enters the service of Cesare Borgia, for whom he draws maps and constructs fortifications. He also meets and befriends Machiavelli, traveling with Borgia as a servant of the Florentine Republic.

1503 Borgia's campaign finished, Leonardo returns to Florence.

1503 Amerigo Vespucci, a Florentine explorer and acquaintance of Leonardo, publishes an account of his voyages sailing west from Europe across the Atlantic. Vespucci's title: *Mundus Novus,* or *New World.* Unlike Columbus, Vespucci understands this new land is not part of Asia.

1503–1506 Leonardo paints a second *Virgin of the Rocks,* which now hangs in the National Gallery in London.

c1503–1504 Leonardo begins to paint the *Mona Lisa.*

October 1503 Leonardo, commissioned to paint a battle scene for Florence's Palazzo Vecchio, chooses a Florentine victory over the Milanese in 1440. The unfinished painting remained on the wall, deteriorating due to Leonardo's experimental methods, for about 60 years. We know what it might have looked like from copies made by other artists.

1504 Michelangelo completes a beautiful sculpture of *David,* the young man in the story of David and Goliath. Leonardo serves on the committee deciding where the statue will be placed in Florence.

1504 Raphael, a 21-year-old artist, moves to Florence. He studies and learns from both Leonardo and Michelangelo.

1505 Leonardo's studies of flight and designs for flying machines abruptly end in his notes.

1506 Pope Julius II employs the architect Bramante, who worked with Leonardo under Ludovico, to begin the reconstruction of Saint Peter's, a church that has stood in the Vatican since the 4th century.

1506 Leonardo sets out for Milan for a brief visit but stays there for seven years. He meets Francesco Melzi, a young nobleman who will become his pupil, friend, and companion. Leonardo paints and studies anatomy.

1509 Publication of *Divina Proportione,* by the mathematician Pacioli, with illustrations by Leonardo

c1510 Leonardo works on another painting that will remain unfinished, *Virgin and Child with St. Anne.* It hangs today in the Louvre.

1512 Michelangelo completes his frescoes on the ceiling of the Sistine Chapel in the Vatican in Rome. The scenes painted on the chapel's ceiling gorgeously illustrate moments and people from the Bible's Old Testament.

1513 Leonardo sets out for Rome with Melzi and Salai.

c1513–1516 Leonardo works on what will be his final painting, a dramatic portrait of John the Baptist. It hangs today in the Louvre.

c1512–1514 Leonardo draws his self-portrait in red chalk. Though other images of him exist, this picture is our only authentic likeness of Leonardo. He shows us the craggy face of an old man with flowing beard, set mouth, and eyes gazing into the distance.

1516 Leonardo goes to France with Melzi, Salai, and all of his possessions.

May 2, 1519 Leonardo dies. He leaves his notebooks to Francesco Melzi and most of his paintings to Salai.

1525–1530 Giacomo (Salai) dies. The King of France finally has the opportunity to buy the paintings Leonardo left to Salai. Today some of them can be found in the Louvre, in Paris.

1570 Francesco Melzi dies in Milan. His heirs allow the scattering of Leonardo's notebooks over the next several centuries. The histories behind the surviving notes are colorful. Pompeo Leoni, a sculptor employed by the King of Spain, managed to acquire a great number of the loose sheets. He cut them up and pasted the scraps onto large pieces of paper, sorting Leonardo's writings by topic and binding them into two large volumes. One of these, containing four hundred sheets of notes and more than seventeen hundred drawings, is now known as the *Codex Atlanticus.* This found its way to Milan and was held there in the Ambrosiana Library until 1796, when Napoleon Bonaparte included it and other Leonardo manuscripts in spoils he brought back to France. Bonaparte explained, "All men of genius…are French, whatever the country which has given them birth." In 1815, at the end of the Napoleonic Wars, the *Codex Atlanticus* was returned to Milan; other Leonardo manuscripts brought back by Napoleon remain in the Institut de France. In the 1760s, the royal librarian discovered Leonardo's notes on anatomy in a trunk in England's Kensington Palace. They are now displayed at Windsor Palace, in England. In 1965, a large stack of notes, lost since 1866, were found in the National Library in Milan. These pages helped scholars learn much more about Leonardo's years in Milan. It is possible that recovery of the scattered notebooks will continue.

1651 Leonardo's *Treatise on Painting,* organized by Melzi, is published. The wide circulation of his theories and practical advice concerning painting reinforces the idea of Leonardo as primarily a painter.

1880s Compilations of Leonardo's notebooks are published and widely studied for the first time. His talent is rapidly recognized to be much more universal than was previously understood, encompassing a seemingly endless field of endeavor and achievement. Leonardo da Vinci's life and mind begin to be regarded as the epitome of human genius.

BIBLIOGRAPHY

Quotes from Leonardo's writings are taken from a variety of the sources listed below.

Bambach, Carmen C., ed. *Leonardo da Vinci: Master Draftsman.* New York: The Metropolitan Museum of Art, 2003. A large, up-to-date catalogue of a spring 2003 show of Leonardo's drawings.

Bramly, Serge. *Discovering the Life of Leonardo da Vinci: A Biography.* Translated by Sian Reynolds. New York: HarperCollins, 1991. Detailed account of Leonardo da Vinci's life and personality.

Brown, David Alan. *Leonardo da Vinci: Origins of a Genius.* New Haven: Yale Univ. Press, 1998. Focuses on the early years of Leonardo's art.

Cooper, Margaret. *The Inventions of Leonardo da Vinci.* New York: Macmillan, 1965. Detailed information on Leonardo's clock, piston, flying machines, construction, and measuring devices.

Gelb, Michael J. *How to Think Like Leonardo da Vinci: Seven Steps to Genius Every Day.* New York: Delacorte Press, 1998. How Leonardo's all-encompassing vision of life can be used in living successfully in today's world.

Hartt, Frederick. *History of Italian Renaissance Art: Painting, Sculpture, Architecture.* Second Edition. Englewood Cliffs, NJ: Prentice-Hall, and New York: Abrams, 1979. Contains a helpful discussion of the *Last Supper.*

Holt, Elizabeth Gilmore, ed. *A Documentary History of Art.* Volume I: *The Middle Ages & the Renaissance.* Illustrated. Garden City, NY: Doubleday, 1957.

Janson, H. W. *History of Art: A Survey of the Major Visual Arts from the Dawn of History to the Present Day.* Second Edition. New York: Abrams, 1977.

Kelen, Emery, ed. and annotator. *Fantastic Tales, Strange Animals, Riddles, Jests, and Prophecies of Leonardo da Vinci.* New York: Thomas Nelson, 1971. A look at Leonardo as Master of Pageants.

MacCurdy, Edward, ed. *The Notebooks of Leonardo da Vinci.* New York: George Braziller, 1958. A massive volume containing all of Leonardo's known writing as of 1958.

McClanathan, Richard B. K. *Leonardo da Vinci.* New York: Abrams, 1990. Good material on Leonardo's birth and youth.

The Notebooks of Leonardo da Vinci. Selection by Pamela Taylor. New York: Mentor, 1960.

Plumb, J. H. *The Horizon Book of the Renaissance.* Edited by Richard M. Ketcham. New York: American Heritage, 1961. Excellent source for life in the Renaissance.

Reti, Ladislao, ed. *Leonardo the Artist, Leonardo the Inventor, Leonardo the Scientist.* 3 volumes. New York: McGraw-Hill, 1980. Information on Luca Pacioli and Leonardo's bridges, forts, alphabet, horse drawings, bicycle, weapons, and studies on water.

Stites, Raymond S. *The Sublimations of Leonardo da Vinci.* Washington, D.C.: Smithsonian Institution Press, 1970. A scholarly treatment of the artist.

Turner, A. Richard. *Inventing Leonardo.* Berkeley: University of California Press, 1994. Treats the changing image of Leonardo through the ages.

Vallenin, Antonina. *Leonardo da Vinci: The Tragic Pursuit of Perfection.* New York: Viking Press, 1938. Romantic biography of Leonardo.

Vollmer, Emil, ed. *Leonardo da Vinci.* New York: Reynal & Company, Inc., 1956. Originally published in Italy by the Istituto Geografico De Agostini, Milan, 1938. Contains reproductions of all of Leonardo's paintings and all drawings of consequence. (My most valuable reference.)

Wallace, Robert, and editors of Time-Life Books. *The World of Leonardo, 1452–1519.* New York: Time-Life Books, 1966. Detailed account of Leonardo da Vinci's life, work, and times.

White, Michael. *Leonardo: The First Scientist.* New York: St. Martin's, 2000. Describes Leonardo as the first true scientific observer.

Zöllner, Frank. *Leonardo da Vinci: 1452–1519.* Cologne, Germany: Taschen, 2000.

HELPFUL REFERENCES FOR ILLUSTRATIONS

Coughlan, Joseph. *Inside the Vatican.* New York: W. H. Smith Publishers, Inc., 1990.

Fusi, Rolando. *Looking at Florence.* Florence: Bonechi Editore, 1972.

Hay, Denys, ed. *The Age of the Renaissance.* New York, Toronto, London, Sydney: McGraw-Hill, 1967. Excellent photo, print, and painting reproductions for historical costume and architectural reference.

Pucci, Eugenio. *All Rome and the Vatican.* Florence: Bonechi Editore, 1975.

WORLD WIDE WEB RESOURCES

A wealth of information via the Internet can be found by searching under the name Leonardo da Vinci. The Boston Museum of Science and the American Museum of Natural History have hosted excellent exhibitions of Leonardo's work. Information can be found on their respective websites at: http://www.mos.org/leonardo/museum.html and http://www.amnh.org/exhibitions/codex/. Also, http://www.mos.org/sln/Leonardo/ features classroom activities.

FOR CHILDREN AND YOUNG ADULTS

Anholt, Laurence. *Leonardo and the Flying Boy: A Story About Leonardo da Vinci.* New York: Barron's, 2000. Fictionalized story about Leonardo and Zoro, his young pupil.

Fritz, Jean. *Leonardo's Horse.* New York: Putnam, 2001. The story of a modern attempt to create Leonardo's Horse in Milan.

Herbert, Janis. *Leonardo da Vinci for Kids: His Life and Ideas.* Chicago: Chicago Review Press, 1998. Art and science explored in an activity book.

Langley, Andrew. *Eyewitness: Leonardo & His Times.* NY: DK Publishing, 2000.

Leonardo da Vinci. New York: Abrams Books for Young Readers, 1990.

Muhlberger, Richard. *What Makes a Leonardo a Leonardo?* New York: Viking and the Metropolitan Museum of Art, 1994.

Stanley, Diane. *Leonardo da Vinci.* New York: Morrow Junior Books, 1996. A picture-book biography.

Visconti, Guido. *The Genius of Leonardo.* Translated by Mark Roberts, illustrated by Bimba Landmann. New York: Barefoot Books, 2000. Fictionalized story of Leonardo and his unruly apprentice, Salai.

Williams, Jay. *Leonardo da Vinci.* New York: American Heritage, 1965. Leonardo's life and work, with excellent "models" of his inventions.

For Tracy

Published in the United States by Dutton Children's Books,
a division of Penguin Young Readers Group
345 Hudson Street, New York, New York 10014
www.penguin.com

Designed by Robert Byrd, Sara Reynolds,
and Richard Amari

Manufactured in China
First Edition

3 5 7 9 10 8 6 4

Library of Congress Cataloging-in-Publication Data
Byrd, Robert.
Leonardo, beautiful dreamer / Robert Byrd.
p. cm.
Summary: Illustrations and text portray the life of Leonardo da Vinci,
who gained fame as an artist, through such works as the *Mona Lisa,*
and as a scientist by studying various subjects
including human anatomy and flight.
ISBN 0-525-47033-6
I. Leonardo, da Vinci, 1452-1519—Juvenile literature. 2. Artists—Italy—
Biography—Juvenile literature. [I. Leonardo, da Vinci, 1452-1519. 2. Artists.
3. Scientists.] I. Leonardo, da Vinci, 1452-1519. II. Title.
N6923.L33B97 2003
709'.2—dc21   2003044860

And you, O MAN, who will discern in this work of mine the wonderful works of Nature,
if you think it would be a criminal thing to destroy it, reflect how much more criminal it is to take the life of a man;
and if this, his external form, appears to thee marvelously constructed, remember that it is nothing as compared
with the soul that dwells in that structure; for that indeed, be it what it may, is a thing divine.
Leave it then to dwell in His work at His good will and pleasure, and let not your rage or malice destroy a life—
for indeed, he who does not value it, does not himself deserve it.

If the painter wishes to see beauties that charm him it lies in his power to create them,

and if he wishes to see monstrosities that are frightful, buffoonish,

or ridiculous, or pitiable, he can be lord and God thereof.

The painter contends with and rivals nature.

I am addressing not those who wish to make money from art but those who expect honor and glory from it.

O Painter! Beware lest the lust of gain should supplant in you the dignity of art;

for the acquisition of glory is a much greater thing than the glory of riches.

That is not riches, which may be lost; virtue is our true good and the true reward of its possessor.

That cannot be lost; that never deserts us, but when life leaves us. As to property and external riches,

hold them with trembling; they often leave their possessor in contempt, and mocked at for having lost them.

When fortune comes, seize her firmly by the forelock, for, I tell you, she is bald at the back.

Iron rusts when it is not used; stagnant water loses its purity

and freezes over with cold; so, too, does inactivity sap the vigor of the mind.

I would prefer to lose the power of movement than that of usefulness. I would prefer death to inactivity.

The desire to know is natural to good men.

The knowledge of all things is possible.

Obstacles cannot crush me. Every obstacle yields to stern resolve. He who is fixed to a star does not change his mind.

I want to work miracles!

Because of their ambition, some men will wish to rise to the sky, but the excessive weight of their limbs will hold them down.